FOR FELIX

First published in the USA 1971
by Thomas Y Crowell Company New York
First published in Great Britain 1971
by Hamish Hamilton Children's Books
27 Wrights Lane London W8 5TZ

Copyright © 1971 Eric Carle

Reissued in revised format 1987

British Library Cataloguing in Publication Data

Carle, Eric
    Do you want to be my friend?
    I. Title
    813'.54 [J]   PZ7

ISBN 0−241−02043−3

Printed in Germany

DO YOU WANT TO BE MY FRIEND?

BY ERIC CARLE

HAMISH HAMILTON, LONDON

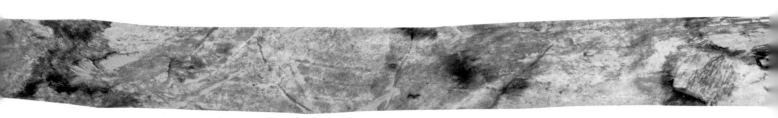